E   Heller, Linda

Trouble at Goodewoode
Manor

8316834

LINDA HELLER

Trouble at Goodewoode Manor

MACMILLAN PUBLISHING CO., INC.
New York
COLLIER MACMILLAN PUBLISHERS
London

8316834

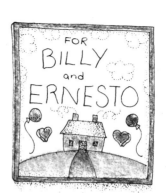

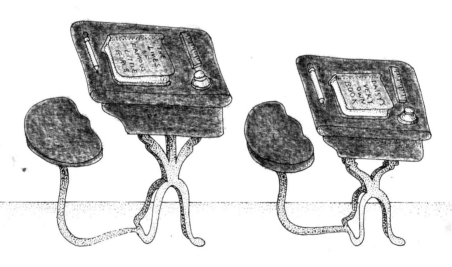

Daisy and Arabella's mother's third cousin once removed was the Queen, and royal blood flowed gently through their veins. They wore the finest dresses, had the best toys, and lived in a house that was so large they never had to play in the same place twice. They even had their very own teacher, Miss Dovecroft, and their very own schoolroom.

"My girls are nearly as graceful as swans and sing almost as sweetly as angels," said Miss Dovecroft during their one o'clock voice lesson.

At two o'clock, fresh air being important, Daisy and
Arabella's little pony April and their pony cart were brought
round. The girls were helped in, and Cook rushed over
with hampers full of tangerine cream tarts, candied
rose petals, and fresh lemonade.

"My little girls are leaving," said Miss Dovecroft,
dabbing her eyes with a white linen hanky.

"Good-bye, good-bye," called Daisy as Arabella guided
April down the path. They were going for a ride around
the house and wouldn't be back until tea.

The trip was quite pleasant until the cart hit a bump.
Daisy and Arabella flew up in the air, sank to the
ground, and watched April and the pony cart disappear
down the path without them.

"I'm afraid we shall have to continue on foot," said Arabella.

"Oh, I so hate changes of plans," said Daisy as tiny tears began to roll down her cheeks.

Suddenly the sky darkened, there was a great crack of thunder, and it started to rain.

"Hurry, Daisy," said Arabella, gathering the baskets and running toward the house. The girls climbed through the nearest open window and found themselves in an enormous room they had never seen before. It was filled almost entirely by a bed.

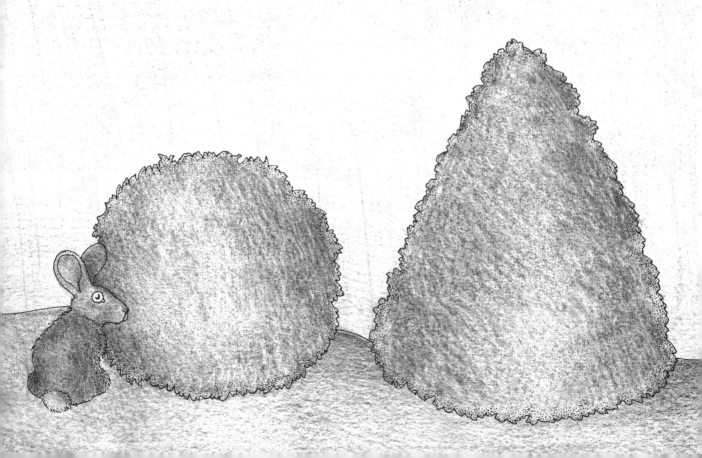

"This must be the bed that was built especially for the visit of King Ethelbault the Immense in 1662," said Arabella. "And even though we shouldn't walk on beds, today we must if we're to be back in time for tea."

The girls bounced across, and by the time they had reached the other side, Arabella had almost perfected a front flip. Then they climbed down and went into the hall.

"I'm certain the parlor is just to the left," said
Arabella, heading in that direction. She opened fifteen
different doors and saw fifteen rooms she'd never seen
before. Daisy then suggested they look to the right.

So they changed directions, went around six corners, and couldn't even find King Ethelbault's room again.

"I'm afraid the worst thing that could have happened has happened," said Arabella, gravely. "We're lost inside Goodewoode Manor."

"I want to go home," sobbed Daisy.

"You are home," said Arabella.

"Oh," said Daisy. "That makes me feel better."

"When one is lost," said Arabella with authority, "one can find one's way by looking at the North Star."

The North Star wasn't in the hallway.

"Or," she continued, "by looking for a path marked by broken branches."

There weren't any branches, either.

"Or," said Daisy, her voice quivering slightly, "by studying a map."

"That's it!" cried Arabella, ripping March 24th out of her diary. "We'll make a map and study it." Arabella drew two little hearts and wrote under them: *Daisy and Arabella are standing right here.* Then she made a dotted line and added: *And this is where they are going.*

With map in hand, the girls went down a narrow stairway. Soon, they heard strange sounds that got louder and louder as they went lower and lower.

"I don't think this is the way to the parlor," said Daisy.

"I don't, either," said Arabella. "This must lead to the dungeon. And I fear we're in the presence of ghosts. We must be hearing the voices of our famous ancestors who came to terrible ends here."

Daisy would go no further, but Arabella continued down the steps, cautiously opened the door, and peeked inside. "Our ancestors," she said," must have been chickens."

Daisy looked in. "Excuse me," she said, "but these aren't ghosts *or* ancestors. They're the dear little chicks I was given last Easter. Olympia, Clarisse, are you lost, too? Arabella will put you on the map so we can rescue you later."

Daisy and Arabella went upstairs to continue their
search for the parlor.

"Our map is almost filled up and we're still lost,"
said Daisy. "Do you think we should call for help?"

"Super idea! But girls with voices lovely as ours
should sing for help," said Arabella.

Daisy and Arabella sang as loudly as they could:

Oh, we're poor little girls who've lost our way—
Help, help, help.
So please come find us without delay.
Help, help, help.
Hungry, sad, and tired are we,
Hoping to be back in time for tea,
Please come find us immediately—
Help! help! help!

Daisy and Arabella waited to be rescued. But no one
came.

"We shall just have to find the way back ourselves,"
said Arabella. "Perhaps the way back is through here."
She pulled the handle of a small gilt door.

"It's very dark in here," said Arabella as she leaned
over to see a bit better. "Still can't see," she said as she
leaned in even farther. Suddenly, she fell in, and Daisy
had only a moment to grab her ankles before she slid
away. The two sisters sailed down the dark chute
until another door opened. They flew out and landed
in a heap.

"We're still lost," said Daisy.

"And locked in, too," said Arabella, trying the door.

Daisy and Arabella stared longingly through the open window high above their heads. They could see daffodils and neatly cut grass. "We'll never get out," said Arabella, sitting down to cry.

MARCH 24

Daisy and Arabella are standing right here

and this is where they are going

door

library

another door

conservatory

old nursery

chickens

sitting room

bedroom

more doors

taller tower

tower

portrait gallery

help!

bathroom

closet

laundry room

"Let's study our map," said Daisy. "I believe we may be right under the parlor," she said, looking at the only blank spot.

Arabella wasn't listening. She was busy soothing the chickens, who were a bit ruffled by their fall. "Don't feel you have to stay here on our account," she said to them, smoothing their feathers. "It's not your fault that you can fly and we can only jump."

"Exactly!" cried Daisy, running to the washboard and placing it on a stool.

"Arabella, come stand here and hold these sheets," she said. Daisy stood on a stool, jumped high in the air, and landed on the other end of the washboard.

Arabella flew up through the open window.
Then she lowered the sheets and Daisy
climbed up.

"My little girls are back!" cried Miss Dovecroft. "Wherever have you been?"

"Just doing a bit of exploring," said Daisy, carefully tracing their travels on the map.

"My, what brave and clever girls I have!" said Miss Dovecroft. And they all went in for tea.